SHADES

D1424686

Published by Evans Brothers Limited
2A Portman Mansions
Chiltern St
London W1U 6NR

British Library Cataloguing in Publication Data
Orme, Helen
Who cares. - (Shades)
1. Young adult fiction
I. Title
823.9'2 [J]

ISBN 0 237 52625 5

Series Editor: David Orme
Editor: Julia Moffatt
Designer: Rob Walster

Contents

Chapter 1
A New Start

Tara was fifteen – well nearly. That's what she told everyone, except that sometimes she told them she was seventeen.

She wasn't afraid of anybody but she hated a lot of people. She hated teachers, social workers, all busybodying people who tried to tell her what to do. Most of all, this morning, she hated her mum.

'You've got to go,' said Mum. 'It's your last chance.'

'I ent going. You can't make me.'

'You've got to. You know what'll happen if you don't.'

'I hate school – I'm going out!'

Her mum caught her by the arm as she made for the door. She shook Tara hard.

'You're going. It ain't school anyway – it's special, and if you don't go they'll put me in prison!'

Tara gave in. She knew there was no way she could get away from Mum while she was in this sort of mood. She got her jacket and her bag and followed her mum out of the door. She wouldn't stay. They couldn't make her. No school she had been to so far had managed that.

Her mum was right. It wasn't a school. It had been for a long time, but now most of

the old Victorian infant school had been
pulled down. All that was left was the hall.
Now, that was being used by the Unit.

The Unit had a posh-sounding name
but everyone knew it was just a dumping
ground for kids who had been thrown
out of school. It didn't need a posh name –
it was just the Unit.

Tara followed her mum in. She didn't
really like meeting new people. She put on
her tough 'you can't get to me' face.

Inside, the building was better than it
had looked from the outside. It was brightly
painted and the walls were covered with
examples of work. Just like any other
school, thought Tara.

The hall was really one big space, but
it had been divided into smaller rooms by
flimsy walls. There was a reception area
by the door with an empty room next to it.

On the other side was an office. The rest of the space was taken up with two classrooms.

The secretary was a thin, rather harassed-looking lady.

'Please sit down. I will see if Mrs Pearson is ready to see you.'

Tara's mum sat down, but Tara just turned her back on the secretary. She wasn't going to do anything anyone told her in this place.

'Please come in.'

A smartly-dressed lady with a welcoming smile stood at the door of the office. The secretary sat back down behind her desk. She looked relieved to have something to hide behind.

Tara's mum went into the office, with Tara dragging behind.

'Please sit down,' said the woman, still

smiling. 'We've got a lot to talk about.'

She looked directly at Tara. 'Hello, my name is Mrs Pearson, and I am the Unit head. You'll meet the other teachers and the rest of the pupils later.'

She was just going to say something else when suddenly there was a shout from one of the bigger rooms.

'—off!' yelled a boy's voice and a door slammed so violently that the office wall shook.

Chapter Two

A Different Type of School

Tara sucked in her breath and waited for the explosion. She would enjoy that. It was always fun when teachers lost their rag. She'd done this sort of thing lots of times in her various schools. They always reacted. They just couldn't help themselves. It gave Tara a sense of real power. It was like pushing a button.

But it didn't happen this time. A lady teacher came out of the room and followed the boy as he stormed out of the building. Another teacher, a man, just carried on with the lesson. Some of the kids were laughing, but no one made it into a big deal.

'Don't worry about that,' said Mrs Pearson. 'Charles gets wound up very easily. Ms Sims will find out what's upset him. Now, let's worry about you.'

'You gonna let him get away with that?' said Tara. 'In my last school he'd have bin sent out.'

'Well, he's put himself out, hasn't he?' smiled Mrs Pearson. 'And, no, I only step in for serious things.'

Tara wondered what might be serious in this place. It was obvious that it wasn't going to be like normal school.

'Now,' said Mrs Pearson, turning to Tara's mum. 'You have read our School Contract document, haven't you?'

'Yeah.'

'Was everything quite clear? Do you have any questions?'

'Yeah. I mean, no.' Tara's mum was getting confused now. 'That's fine.'

'Have you discussed it with Tara?'

'No point,' said Mrs Varley. 'She never listens to anything I say.'

'But it affects her. She must understand what we are asking her to do. She has got to agree too, or we can't offer her a place.'

Mrs Varley shrugged her shoulders. Mrs Pearson looked at them both and thought just how much Tara looked like her mum.

She looked back to Tara.

'You must agree to attend regularly. You

must agree to work hard and co-operate with the staff, and you must not come into the Unit under the influence of drink or drugs.'

Tara glared at her. She hated people who said 'you must' and 'you must not'.

'I don't do drugs,' she said. 'I'm not stupid!'

'I know you're not,' said Mrs Pearson. 'I've had reports from your previous schools. That's not the point. Do you understand our rules?'

'S'pose so.'

'Will you agree to them?

'S'pose so.'

'In that case, welcome to the Unit. You can start tomorrow morning.'

The next morning there was another battle between Tara and her mum. Tara finally gave in when Mum threatened to drag her to the Unit. She didn't want to arrive on

her first day with her mum holding her
hand.

She left home in plenty of time, but she
dawdled so it was well after nine o'clock
by the time she arrived. Mrs Pearson was
watching from her office. She went out as
soon as she saw Tara.

'We were getting worried about you.
Your mum said you left home ages ago.'

Tara was startled.

'We always check on absences,' said
Mrs Pearson. 'If you don't arrive within ten
minutes of the start of the morning session,
I ring your home. Now let me introduce you
to the rest of the staff and pupils.'

'Great,' thought Tara. 'Checking up all
the time. I might as well be in prison. They
won't stop me though – I'll do what I want
to do, not what they want!'

Chapter Three
I Don't Want to be Here

Mrs Pearson opened the door to one of the classrooms. There were three teachers and six pupils. She introduced the teachers.

'Mrs Mansell, Mr Dale and Ms Sims are here all the time,' she said. 'We usually work in two groups, one for key stage 3, and one for key stage 4. Whichever teacher is not with a group is on hand to work with people on their own.'

'Hello,' said the older woman, Mrs Mansell. 'Do you want everyone to introduce themselves?'

Tara looked round at the pupils. There was one other girl and five boys. The girl and one of the boys looked about her own age. The other four boys were older.

'I'm glad you're here,' said Mr Dale. 'We can go next door and make a start. Come on Lisa and Mickey.'

Mickey grinned at Tara but the girl, Lisa, looked at her with a scowl. She turned to follow Mr Dale and shoved Tara aside as she went through the door.

Tara lost her temper.

'You watch it, you cow!'

'Or what? What you gonna do?'

Mr. Dale moved over to Lisa.

'Come on Lisa – you never know – you might even get to like each other.'

'My name's Leez, not Lisa – how many times do I have to say it? And she's skank. I'm never gonna be friends with her!'

'OK, then. You can sit at opposite ends of the table. Mickey and I will sit in between you.'

Mr Dale exchanged a glance with the other two teachers.

'I'll come with you this morning,' said Mrs Mansell and followed them into the other room.

Mr Dale found a new folder for Tara and settled them down with some English work. Mrs Mansell sat down with Tara.

'Have a go at this and I'll explain anything you don't understand.'

'I can do it myself,' said Tara. 'I'm not stupid.'

Leez looked up. 'Sez who?'

'If you two are going to carry on like this it's going to be a long morning,' sighed Mr Dale.

''Snot my fault – it's her.'

Mickey decided it was time someone took notice of him.

'I don't want to be in with two girls. Can't I go next door?'

Tara decided not to speak to anyone. She had done this before. It usually got her noticed. If she stopped talking someone always asked her what the matter was. This time it didn't work quite that way. Mrs Mansell offered good advice on the work, which Tara ignored, and Mr Dale concentrated on working with the other two.

Tara was getting really fed up when there was a sudden burst of noise from the room next door. Mrs Mansell looked at her watch.

'Break-time already,' she said. 'Doesn't time fly when you're having fun.'

Mr Dale laughed and opened the door.

'Let's go and join the others,' he said. 'Would you like a hot drink, Tara?'

Leez and Mickey went into the other room. Leez went over to one of the boys and started whispering to him. They both looked at Tara and laughed.

'Do you want tea or coffee?' asked Ms Sims.

Tara stood to one side holding her mug. She hated it here. She especially hated that girl Lisa.

Then Leez laughed again. The boy she was talking to pretended to fall against another and pushed him into Tara. Coffee went everywhere.

Tara knew who had planned it, and leapt over to Leez to grab her hair. Leez was ready for her. She moved to one side and stuck out her leg. Tara tripped and banged the side of her face against the table. She was really angry now.

There was no one close enough to hit. She looked towards the door. Mrs Pearson was coming into the room. Tara pushed her to one side and ran out.

She had to get away. She was never coming back again.

Chapter Four
A Day Off

Her mum wasn't in when she got home. The house was cold so Tara went upstairs and got into bed. She was not going back to the Unit, that was for sure.

The phone rang. She ignored it. It was probably that stupid Mrs Pearson. The phone rang again a couple of times later in the afternoon, but she still ignored it.

Luckily it was late by the time her mum got home so Tara didn't need to tell her anything.

The next day she got up as usual and pretended to get ready for school. She knew now that they would ring when she didn't turn up, but by that time she would be a long way away.

Her mum wasn't paying much attention to Tara. She was slumped in front of the telly with a cup of black coffee. Tara looked round for her mum's bag. Opening it, she found a roll of notes stuffed down inside. She took the whole roll but didn't bother to look for coins. Her mum might have heard the chink in spite of the state she was in. With luck she might not even remember how much she had had. Still, who cared if she did? Tara certainly didn't!

Tara decided to head for the town centre. As she sat on the bus she watched the streams of kids heading to school. She even caught sight of Mickey and that other boy, Charles, Mrs Pearson had called him.

'Stupid things,' she thought. 'I'm not going back to that place. I hate school. Still they'll probably chuck me out now.'

She smiled at the thought. Her mum would moan; she always moaned about everything.

She got off the bus and decided to go round the shops, but it was still early and half of them were still closed. She bought something to eat and wandered round to the park. She'd be able to sit there while she decided what to do.

'Hello.'

The voice was friendly and sort of familiar. She looked round.

'You don't remember me – it's Liam – I went to Green Lane School with you. What are you doin' here then? Bunking off?'

She remembered him now. He was a few years older than her – she'd been friendly with his younger sister. Until they chucked her out of Green Lane, that was.

'Yeah. I hate school.'

'Me, too,' said Liam. 'I left last summer.' He grinned at her. 'I work for the parks department now – I'm here every day.' He sat down next to her.

He was good for a laugh and Tara would have been happy to have stayed there all morning, but some bloke arrived and told him to get back to work. Tara was surprised when Liam got up with a grin. He hadn't been like that at school.

'See ya again then?'

'Yeah – maybe.'

She decided to head for the arcade. She'd lost interest in the shops. Shops needed a mate to go round with.

The arcade was busy. It was mainly full of youths but there were a few older men as well. There weren't many girls.

One of the older men broke away from his group and wandered over to Tara.

'Hello darlin'. All on your own then?'

Tara smiled sweetly at him. He looked as if he might have money. He could buy her a drink and something to eat.

He grinned back.

'My name's Jeff, by the way. Want a roll-up?'

He took out a small tin and winked slyly at her.

She shook her head. 'Not now, thanks.' She knew what he meant but ignored it.

He looked over towards his mates and cocked his head slightly. They grinned back. One gave him a thumbs-up and they turned away.

'I haven't seen you before,' he said. 'Where've you bin hiding all my life?'

Suddenly there was a noise from near the doors. Jeff looked round.

'Sorry darlin', gotta go – see you around, yeah?' He moved away quickly, and before she could say anything he was out of sight. She looked round. There was a policeman by the door and, of all people, that stupid Mrs Pearson.

Chapter Five
The Drugs Man

'Hello, Tara. I wondered if we might find you here.'

Tara glared furiously at her. In her other schools nobody had bothered finding her when she had bunked off.

Mrs Pearson looked as if she knew what Tara was thinking.

'The Unit isn't like an ordinary school

you know,' she said. 'When I rang your mum she told me she thought you had come to school. We have to know where you are. We're responsible for you during the school day. If you don't turn up we have to take steps to find you.'

'With the pigs!'

'No, the policeman was nothing to do with me. That was just coincidence.'

Tara shrugged.

'What ya gonna do to me now then?'

'Take you back to the Unit,' said Mrs Pearson. 'You can tell me what it's all about on the way back.'

Settled into Mrs Pearson's car it was surprisingly easy to tell her all about it. Mrs Pearson didn't go on like most teachers. She really listened.

'They all hate me! That Leez girl is the worst. She made them all laugh at me. She's a real bitch.'

'I don't talk about people behind their backs,' said Mrs Pearson. 'But since she's told everybody all about it, I suppose I can tell you. She was in a bad mood yesterday because she'd had a blazing row with her foster mum the night before. Her foster mum rang social services and said she didn't want her back. When Lisa went out, her foster mum threw all her things after her and bolted the door. When she came into school she had no idea where she was going to go that night.'

'What did happen? What was the row about?'

'Social services have found her a temporary place for a week while they fix up something new. I can't discuss anything else with you. But Lisa is much happier today. If you'll try to make a fresh start when we get back, I know she will.'

Tara thought about it. She supposed she could give it a try. She often had rows with her mum, but at least she'd never been told to get out forever.

When they got back to the Unit, Tara was surprised to see that everybody was in the same room. They all looked at her for a moment and she was getting ready to run again. Then two of the boys spoke together.

'Where you bin then?' said Mickey.

'So kind of you to come,' said one of the others, putting on a posh voice. She looked over. It was the boy called Charles.

'Shut up Chaff!' said another voice. 'Leave 'er alone.'

Tara was startled – the new voice was Leez, but sounding as if she meant it.

Tara smiled round. 'Just fancied a morning off.' She shrugged her shoulders

and pulled a face. 'All work and no play –
you know.'

Leez laughed.

'Yeah – know how you feel. Mind you it's
a good thing you came in or you'd have
missed all the fun.'

Tara was just about to ask what fun
when the door opened again. In came Mr
Dale, Ms Sims and another bloke.

Leez moved over to Tara. 'He's fit,'
she said.

Chapter Six
The Real Thing

'Right – settle down, you lot,' said Ms Sims. 'I want to introduce Mr Carter. He's from the drug advisory service.'

'Yeah!' Tony's arm punched the air. 'Go on then – what do you advise?'

'What's the best deal we can get round here?' Dobs called out. 'Do you know that Smithy? He's cheaper than anyone else. Or so he reckons.'

'He might be cheaper,' said Tony. 'But it's not always good – he cuts it.'

Mr Carter smiled at them. 'Hi. My name's Joe,' he said. 'No, I haven't come to tell you where to get drugs. You don't need my help for that.'

Dobs laughed. 'What a prat!' he said. 'You people don't know nuffin'.'

'Once you get started it's difficult to stop,' mimicked Chaff, putting on his posh voice. 'We've heard it all before mate.'

'It takes over your life,' echoed Bozo.

'Think of the cost!' giggled Tara.

'He wouldn't know an eighth if he got it on a plate,' said Tony. 'I bet I could get better quality stuff than he's ever set eyes on.'

But Joe wasn't quite as stupid as they thought he was. He had obviously done this sort of thing before.

He began by telling them about himself.

'I got into this because of my brother. He died when he was seventeen, because he took something someone gave him without checking what it was.'

In spite of themselves they began to get interested.

Joe talked about his brother's addiction, his shoplifting and his eventual death. They could see his emotion as he talked. It made Tara want to cry, but she wouldn't show it. When Joe finished talking about his brother, he reached for his briefcase.

'Before you even think about it,' he said, 'these aren't real. They are just samples to show you what the things look like.'

'Think we don't know?' Bozo muttered.

The talk began to get boring after that. They soon began to get restless.

At the end of the session they were left to themselves.

Tony pulled out a packet of cigarette papers and a small tin.

'Want some?' he said, flashing them around the group.

'You haven't got it here?' said Tara in surprise. 'I thought we weren't allowed to.'

'Don't be stupid,' said Tony. 'How are they going to find out?'

Bozo laughed.

'Do you always do what you're told, then?'

'Miss Goody-goody,' sneered Leez.

'Course I don't,' flashed Tara. 'I do what I want, not what other people tell me.'

'Good,' said Tony. 'Want some of this then? I can get plenty more.'

Ms Sims came back in just then, so Tara didn't have to answer. She looked sharply at Tony. He grinned back at her. His hands were firmly in his pockets.

At the end of the day Chaff came up to Tara.

'What're you doin' tonight then?'

'Dunno.'

'Wanna come with us then? We're going down the arcade.'

Tara knew she had to go. If she refused the offer of friendship, life at the Unit would be a real drag.

Anyway it might be fun.

Chapter Seven
New Friends

'I'm goin' out tonight.'

'Where to? Take your key and don't be late home.'

Tara knew it didn't really matter what time she got home. It was Friday night. Her mum wouldn't be back until the early hours. That was if she came home at all.

'I'm goin' round to a mate's house – one

of the boys from the Unit.'

'Just don't be too late, right?'

'Right!'

Tara left just before her mum. No chance of money tonight but she still had plenty left from the night before.

They had arranged to meet at Chaff's house. It wasn't far away from Tara's. Leez was already there when she arrived. So was Tony.

'Come on,' said Leez. She and Chaff were giggling. 'Come upstairs.'

Tara had just got to the top of the stairs when Bozo arrived, carrying a two-litre plastic bottle of lemonade. Tara was surprised – she couldn't see Bozo as a lemonade drinker.

'Great!' laughed Tony. 'Now we can really get into it.'

Leez looked at Tara.

'It's for a bong,' she said. 'It's much better if you do it this way – it's stronger and quicker.'

Tara realised it was going to be difficult to pretend that she knew as much as the others. She had never even smoked the stuff, let alone done anything else, but she didn't want the others to know. They would only mock her for being a goody-goody.

'I've never done it that way.' She shrugged her shoulders. 'But if it's as good as you say…'

It was very late when she got home but her mum wasn't in. She felt great. She had never been so relaxed.

She couldn't see why people made so much fuss about drugs. She had never felt this good about things in her whole life.

Next morning was Saturday. She wasn't sure what she was going to do with the day but she was sure about the evening. She would be out with Leez and Chaff again. She couldn't wait.

There was no sign of Mum when she got downstairs but her bag was there so she must be home. Tara didn't bother to wake her. She didn't want any questions about her own plans.

She searched her mum's bag for more money. There were a few coins loose at the bottom of the bag, which she took. That'd pay her bus fare. She was going to get out of the house and stay out. She couldn't go round to Chaff's place until later.

On the bus she started to plan the day. She thought about Liam. It had been good talking to him. He had shown he liked her. She would go down to the park and see if he was there.

He was there, but not working. He was just sitting on a bench watching the pigeons. She wandered over to him, trying to seem casual.

'Hiya. Not working today then?'

'I'm glad you came,' he said, not pretending at all. 'What do you want to do then?'

'Let's go and eat.'

Over the burger and chips they talked about old times.

'What happened to you then?' asked Tara bluntly.

Liam looked embarrassed.

'I was away,' he said. 'I got done for car theft and sent to a young offenders' place for six months.'

'I always thought that you were dead

straight,' said Tara. 'You never went in for nicking much.'

'Got into drugs, didn't I? Met this guy who needed cars and paid well if I did the dirty work for him.'

'Do you still do drugs?' said Tara. She was about to tell him about her own experiences the night before.

'No way. It's a real mug's game. The young offenders' programme sorted me. I got this job and I'm gonna stay clean.'

She decided to shut up.

They spent the rest of the day together. Tara really liked him. He was good fun, and much kinder than the boys at the Unit.

'What about tonight?' he said.

'Sorry can't – got something else on. How about tomorrow?'

Chapter Eight
Don't Do It!

Life was definitely on the up for Tara. She had got used to being at the Unit. The other kids were OK, most of the time. Sometimes they were fun; other times things went wrong, and there were rows. Leez, especially, was very moody, but Tara was getting used to that.

And there was Liam. After their meeting

in the park, she'd met up with Liam more and more often, and now they were an item. He made her feel special.

The other thing that made life bearable was the drugs. It had been so good that first time that she had joined in whenever the others asked her.

Chaff wouldn't give her any more for free, but he was happy if she paid for it. At first it was just at the weekends, usually in Chaff's house, but sometimes in other places. Tara was sure she could handle it. It made her much calmer. She could cope with her mum's moods and ignore things she didn't like.

It was Chaff's idea to take her to the arcade.

'You need to get your own stuff,' he said. 'I need mine. I'll take you to meet Smithy.

Meet you down there tonight – about half-nine.'

Tara was stressed when she met Liam later that afternoon. Chaff had refused to give her anything, not even enough for one smoke. She was going to have to go and meet Chaff soon.

'I gotta go early tonight,' she said, hoping he wouldn't ask questions.

But he did. He wanted to know why and where. It was just like her mum.

In the end she stormed off and left him. It was the easiest way. She didn't want more hassle. She just wanted to be left alone to live her own life.

It was nearly ten by the time she got to the arcade, and she was worried that Chaff wouldn't be there.

She looked anxiously round, then saw Chaff and Bozo in a huddle with a couple of other guys. She felt in her pocket to make sure her money was still there and walked over to them.

'Hiya,' she said.

'Well, well,' said one. 'Fancy meeting you again.'

'You know her, Smithy?' said Bozo.

'We've met,' he grinned.

'Hello, Jeff.'

'What can I do for you this time then?'

'I want some stuff – you know.'

'OK, but not here. The management watches us. Meet you out the back in five minutes.'

He turned away and began to talk to his mates. Tara wandered off and made her way casually to the door.

She didn't have to wait long. Jeff soon followed and the little packet was safe in her pocket.

'What do you think you're playing at?'

It was a moment or two before she recognised the harsh voice. It was Liam, but looking like she'd never seen him before. He was furious.

'Haven't you listened to anything I've told you? You know what this stuff does to you.'

He tried to grab the packet. She pulled her hand away.

'You can't tell me what to do!' she said angrily. 'What's it got to do with you anyway?'

Chapter Nine
A Night Out

It was going to be a good night. Tara had made up her mind. No rows. She would keep off the drugs. She'd just had one toke before she left home. That would keep her going. Liam would never know.

Although Liam had made so much fuss when he discovered what she was doing, they were closer than ever now. She sometimes wished he wasn't so special to her. She had to pretend she was using less than she was. She wanted to stop, she really did.

He still kept on at her to give it up completely. Sometimes it got too much and she would just walk away. He didn't get it. Just because he'd given it up, he couldn't see why she needed it. It wasn't doing any harm. She could handle it.

It was Liam's eighteenth birthday. He was going to take her to a club. He'd even fixed it to get her some ID. She knew that when she was dressed up, she easily looked about eighteen.

The club was dark, the music was loud and it was very exciting. Liam seemed quite at home. She hadn't realised he was into the club scene.

It got hotter and hotter. Tara wished she

had something to keep her going. Some of the other people there looked as if they would be able to keep going all night.

Liam went off to get more drinks. She knew it would take ages. There were so many people. She looked round the room. Surely that was Jeff? Yes. Did she have time to get over to him before Liam came back?

She looked over towards the bar. She couldn't even see Liam. She had plenty of time.

'Hello, Jeff.'

He looked round, surprised. 'Hello darlin'. What d'ya want then?' He grinned at her.

'I just want something to keep me going.'

'I've got just the thing.' He looked round. No one was taking any notice of them. He took out a small packet.

'A couple of these, and you'll never want to stop.'

'What are they? Are they safe?'

'Never mind what – it's good stuff. Go on, have it on me. Gotta go now. Bye.'

He turned and headed off into the crowd, leaving her with the packet in her hand.

She went to the loo. Once she was safely locked in she shook out the contents. There were four tablets.

Jeff hadn't told her how many to take, but he had said they were safe. She was sure he wouldn't give her anything dodgy.

She swallowed two of them and went back out. Just in time. Liam was forcing his way back towards her.

She gave him a big smile.

Chapter Ten
Panic

Liam gave her both drinks to hold and
then headed off again to speak to a mate
he'd just seen. Suddenly Jeff was at her side.

'Know him, don't I? He'd like something,
I'm sure.'

Tara sipped her drink. She shrugged her
shoulders. Jeff grinned and waved his hand
over Liam's glass. Then he disappeared into

the crowd again. She looked at Liam's glass. Had she really just seen what she thought?

Liam came back. He grabbed his glass and drank it straight down. Should she tell him? Why should she? He'd feel as good as her now.

It was great. Tara had never felt so happy. She didn't want it ever to stop. She had so much energy. She could go on dancing all night. She looked over at Liam. He was looking great too.

It was hot in the club and getting hotter. Tara was sweating. The flashing lights were getting brighter. The music was so intense that she just gave herself up to the rhythms.

She looked at Liam again. He looked hot too. He looked back at her and grinned.

'You know something. I've only just

realised. I really love you.'

He had to shout to make himself heard over the music. Tara's heart was pounding, sending the blood rushing to her face.

'I love you, too,' she yelled.

It must be love. She'd never felt like this before.

Liam pulled her close to him. She could feel the heat of his body. He was sweating too. She could feel his heart beating.

'Let's find somewhere a bit quieter,' he mouthed it into her ear.

She nodded and they began to move towards the edge of the room.

The lights were flashing – brighter and brighter. The noise seemed to increase, the music, people's voices, all pushing in on her, making her dizzy. She felt her head spinning, then her whole body seemed to be spinning as well. She stumbled, and fell.

She grabbed at Liam as she went down, pulling him on top of her.

At first no one noticed. Then a couple got so close that the girl nearly tripped over them.

The bloke gave Liam a kick.

'Get up you idiots!'

When there was no reaction he bent closer. The girl looked at Tara's face and started screaming.

It took several minutes before they could get anyone to take much notice. There were plenty of screams anyway; no one paid any attention to them. Then one of the bouncers spotted that something was going on. Three burly blokes moved swiftly in the direction of the fuss. One look was enough.

'Get them out of here – quick!'

One bloke picked up Tara and carried

her towards the door. The other two held Liam between them and dragged him out, trying to make it look as if he was drunk.

The three heavies took them out through a side door into an alleyway, and left them propped up against the smelly wall. They weren't the club's responsibility. They would be found outside and nobody could prove anything.

Tara was making little moaning noises. Her body was still burning hot.

Liam was quite still and silent.

He was getting really cold.

Chapter Eleven
Never Again

Tara gradually became aware of noises around her. There were voices, a sort of electrical humming and hurrying footsteps.

She tried to open her eyes, but the light was too bright. She lay very still trying to remember what had happened.

There was something important, *really* important. Something to do with Liam.

What was it? She couldn't remember.

There were tubes attached to her. Things dragging on her arms. She felt very sore.

There was no going back now though. She was awake and she had to deal with it.

She was madly thirsty. She wriggled and tried to call out. A low moaning noise came from nearby. It took a moment before she realised that she was making the noise.

'Hello dear, how are you feeling?'

What a stupid question, she thought.

'Terrible,' she said.

She tried to open her eyes again. This time she managed to keep them open.

A nurse was standing by her bed, fiddling with a monitor on a stand.

'You've been very lucky,' said the nurse. 'You were in a really bad way when they brought you in.'

'What happened?' She could remember the

noise and the lights. She remembered the way Liam looked at her.

'Where's Liam?'

'I'm afraid I don't really know anything,' said the nurse. 'You'll have to wait for the doctor, or your mum.'

It was some time before anyone else came near her. Nurses rushed about, but apart from the odd glance in her direction, didn't do much. She dozed off again. Thinking was hard work.

'You stupid little cow! You could've killed yourself. What d'ya think you've bin playing at!'

Oh great – it was Mum. Tara opened her eyes warily.

'Where's Liam?'

'You listening to me? If you ever do anything like this again I'll kill you. What were you doin' down by the club? They only let you in if you're eighteen. Who gave you the stuff? Who's Liam? Did you get it from him?'

Questions, questions, questions. Was she ever going to stop?

'Now calm down, Mrs Varley. She's not up to answering too many questions just yet. When she is the police want to talk to her.'

The voice was calm and quiet. The young doctor smiled down at Tara. Then she turned to Tara's mum.

'She was brought in with a young man. Was that Liam?'

Mrs Varley shrugged her shoulders.

'Dunno,' she said. 'She never tells me what she's doin'.'

'Yeah,' said Tara. 'It must have been. We were together all night. Where is he? Can I see him?'

'All in good time,' said the doctor. 'May I talk to you outside, Mrs Varley?' She turned and gently pushed Tara's mum away from the bedside.

Tara watched them go. It was all coming back now. Everything she and Liam had said. The stuff had been great at first but it wasn't so great now. Liam was right. She would tell him so as soon as she saw him. She wouldn't do it again. She knew she could make the break with his help. She really loved him. They could make it work.

Where was he? She needed to see him, to tell him everything.

Her mum and the doctor were coming back. She looked at her mum's face.

'What's up?'

For a moment there was no answer and Tara realised there was something they didn't want to tell her. They hadn't answered her questions. They hadn't said anything about him.

'Liam?'

'I'm so sorry,' said the doctor. 'He—'

Her mum loomed over the bed.

'He's dead, you stupid little cow. Dead! And you nearly died too. It's no more than he deserved. If I had my way they'd string 'em all up. Pushing drugs to kids your age!'

'He was dead when they brought you in last night,' said the doctor gently, glaring at Mrs Varley. 'The dose was too strong. He had a history, you know.'

She couldn't answer. She couldn't believe it. He had tried so hard. He would never have taken anything! What had Jeff given him? Why hadn't she stopped him? It was all her fault.

She rolled herself up into a tight ball.

'Go away. Leave me alone.'

Her mum touched her on the shoulder but the doctor nodded towards the door.

'I'll take care of this – you go and get a cup of tea.'

Tara lay completely still. What was she going to do? What should she say to the police? Should she tell them what she'd seen? What would Jeff do to her if she told? She wouldn't get into as much trouble if she just kept quiet.

Then she thought of Liam. He would get all the blame. It wasn't his fault. It wasn't fair.

There was no going back now, though. She was on her own and she had to deal with it.